Percy, Graham.
The city mouse and the
country mouse / retold and
illustrated by Graham Percy.

The City Mouse and the Country Mouse

RETOLD AND ILLUSTRATED BY GRAHAM PERCY

For Bette

Distributed in the United States of America by
The Child's World®
1980 Lookout Drive • Mankato, MN 56003-1705
800-599-READ • www.childsworld.com

ACKNOWLEDGMENTS
The Child's World®: Mary Berendes, Publishing Director
The Design Lab: Kathleen Petelinsek, Art Direction and Design;
Anna Petelinsek, Page Production

LIBRARY OF CONGRESS CATALOGING-IN-PUBLICATION DATA
Percy, Graham.
The city mouse and the country mouse / retold and illustrated by
Graham Percy.
p. cm. — (Aesop's fables)
Summary: When the town mouse and the country mouse visit each other,
they find they prefer very different ways of life.
ISBN 978-1-60253-198-7 (lib. bound : alk. paper)
[1. Fables. 2. Folklore.] I. Aesop. II. Country mouse and the city mouse.
English. III. Title. IV. Series.
PZ8.2.P435Cg 2009
398.2—dc22
[E] 2009001581

MORAL

A simple, peaceful life is better than a rich one filled with dangers.

There once was a little brown mouse who lived happily among the country bushes. Every day, he roamed the sunny fields. He searched for tasty nuts, berries, and fruits to eat. Every night, he snuggled into his warm bed. The little mouse was happy in his home under an old oak tree.

One day, the country mouse invited his cousin to stay. His cousin was a city mouse. The country mouse made a delicious supper of berries, nuts, and apples. He even gave up his comfortable bed for his city cousin to sleep in.

After only a few days in the country, the city mouse was grumpy.

"I don't know how you can stand living here," he said. "It's boring here. You have to work hard to find every meal. Your bed is lumpy, too. Come back to the city with me. I'll show you what life is really like."

What an adventure! The country mouse was excited. He packed his bags, and the two cousins set off for the city.

The country mouse had never seen anything as large and beautiful as the city mouse's house. The city mouse proudly led his cousin inside. He took him upstairs to a grand dining room.

The country mouse couldn't believe the feast he saw! He followed his city cousin as he picked through bowls of nuts, platters of cheese, and plates of cookies.

"Help yourself," said the city mouse as he climbed onto a plate of cake. "This is how we city mice eat every night."

The country mouse squeaked with delight! He quickly began to nibble on a piece of cheese.

But before the country mouse had taken two bites, he heard a frightening hiss. A large cat had appeared in the room!

The two mice rushed to hide behind a bowl of fruit.

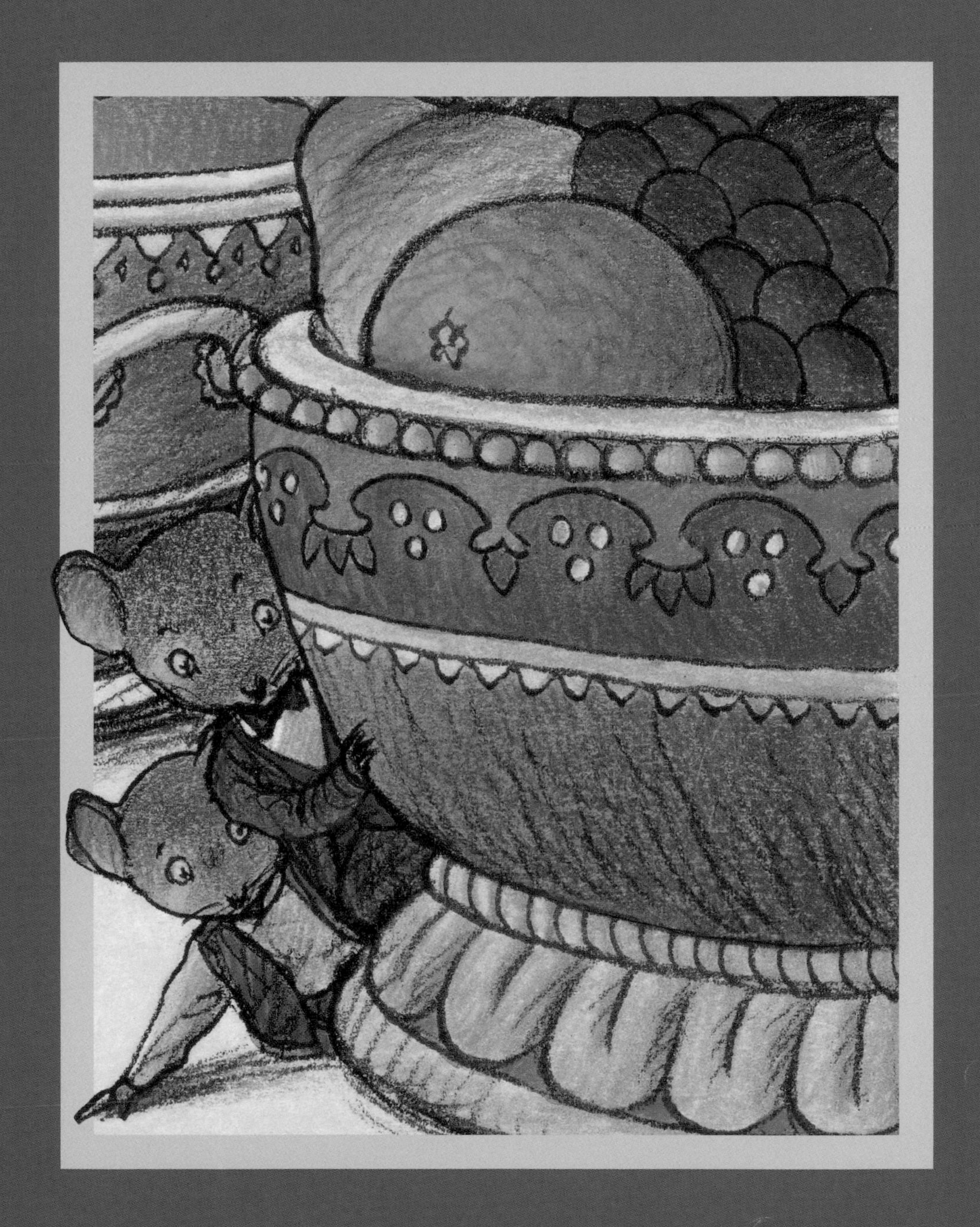

The cat prowled around the table, then left the room. The mice breathed a sigh of relief. After a bit, they carefully crept out of their hiding place.

But just as they were about to start eating again, the mice heard a frightful bark. A huge dog bounded into the room!

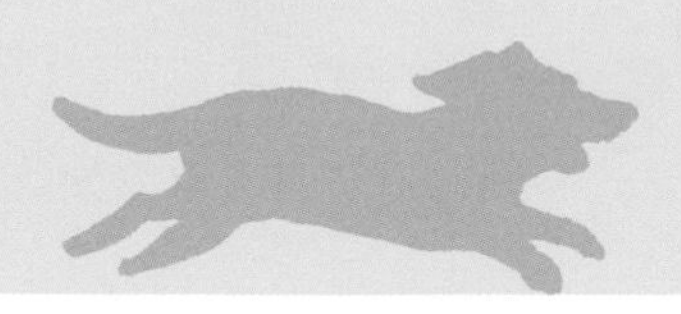

"Oh no!" cried the country mouse. He and the city mouse jumped off the table. They rushed to hide behind a clock on the fireplace.

The dog sniffed around for a long time. After a while, he left the room.

The country mouse had never been so scared in all his life. He shook his head and wiped his brow.

"If this is the way you live every night," he said to his cousin, "then I'm afraid this isn't the life for me. I'm going back to the country right away."

The city mouse sadly reached into his coat pocket. He brought out a tiny pencil and a scrap of paper.

"Please write me a note to remember you by," he said. He handed the pencil and paper to the country mouse.

The country mouse carefully wrote a message. When he was finished, he gave it to the city mouse.

A simple, peaceful life is better than a rich one filled with dangers.

AESOP

Aesop was a storyteller who lived more than 2,500 years ago. He lived so long ago, there isn't much information about him. Most people believe Aesop was a slave who lived in the area around the Mediterranean Sea—probably in or near the country of Greece.

Aesop's fables are known in almost every culture in the world, in almost every language. His fables are even *part* of some languages! Some common phrases come from Aesop's fables, such as "sour grapes" and "Don't count your chickens before they're hatched."

ABOUT FABLES

Fables are one of the oldest forms of stories. They are often short and funny, and have animals as the main characters. These animals act like people. Often, fables teach the reader a lesson. This is called a *moral.* A moral might teach right from wrong, or show how to act in good, kind ways. A moral might show what happens when someone makes a poor decision. Fables teach us how to live wisely.

ABOUT THE ILLUSTRATOR

Graham Percy was a famous illustrator of more than one hundred books. He was born and raised in New Zealand. He first studied art at the Elam School of Art in New Zealand and then moved to London, England, to study at the Royal College of Art.

Mr. Percy especially loved to draw animals, many types of which can be found in his books. He illustrated books on everything from mysteries to lullabies. He was even a designer for the animated film "Hugo the Hippo." Mr. Percy lived most of his life in London.